Boris

The Beetle Who Wouldn't Stay Down

By Hiawyn Oram
with pictures by Tony Ross

Andersen Press
London

First published in Great Britain in 2000 by Andersen Press Ltd., 20 Vauxhall Bridge Road, London SW1V 2SA.
Published in Australia by Random House Australia Pty., 20 Alfred Street, Milsons Point, Sydney, NSW 2061.
All rights reserved. Colour separated in Switzerland by Photolitho AG, Zürich.
Printed and bound in Italy by Grafiche AZ, Verona.

10   9   8   7   6   5   4   3   2   1

British Library Cataloguing in Publication Data available.

ISBN 0 86264 977 3

This book has been printed on acid-free paper

Boris and Ben were two water beetles who lived with their mother at the bottom of the pond.

Every day they asked, "When shall we go up?" And every day Minnie their mother said, "Never. We're bottom-of-the-pond beetles. That's what we are and that's what we'll always be."

But Boris and Ben were curious.
"I have to see what's up there," said Boris.
"Me too!" said Ben.
So without waiting a moment longer, they began to swim up.
Up and further up . . .

. . . until they met Mr Minnow.
"Going u . . . uup?" he asked.
"As fast as possible," said Boris.
"Then take one of my bubbles," said Mr Minnow.

Well, Boris and Ben had never been in a bubble before but in they swam and up they rode.

Up and up. And there, as up as it went, the bubble stopped and the Beetles stepped out . . .

. . . into the midst of a million Tadpoles.

"Is this UP?" enquired Boris.

"Not *right up* up, but it's not far down," said a Tadpole. "And we're on our way to an Up-Here party . . . so why not come along?"

Well, Boris and Ben had never been to a party, up or down, but they joined the Tadpoles and stayed up.

Up they stayed, past midnight . . . past one o'clock . . . past two o'clock . . . past three . . . four . . . five . . .

. . . till the dawn broke and it was day.

"Hey, Tadpoles," said Boris. "For nights like that I could stay up forever. But can you get breakfast up here?"

"At the Surface Café, of course," yawned the Tadpoles.

Well, Boris and Ben had never eaten breakfast out before but off they swam to the Surface Café.

"Now, that's funny," said Boris to the Waitress. "Though this looks up, what's up THERE?"

"Toptoad's territory," said the Waitress. "As up as it gets."

"And no one goes there," said a Floating Boatman. "'Cept Toptoad and Lady Toptoad who ARE there."

"Well, that's where I'm going," said Boris.

"Then better let me take you," said the Boatman. "I know the way."

Well, Boris had never been in a boat, but he was ready. It was Ben who quavered. "Look," he quavered, "we've come up this far, now let's just go home and tell Mother all about it."

"You can," said Boris. "I'M going to the top of the top in this boat."

So while Boris helped prepare the boat, Ben went down . . .

down, down he went . . .

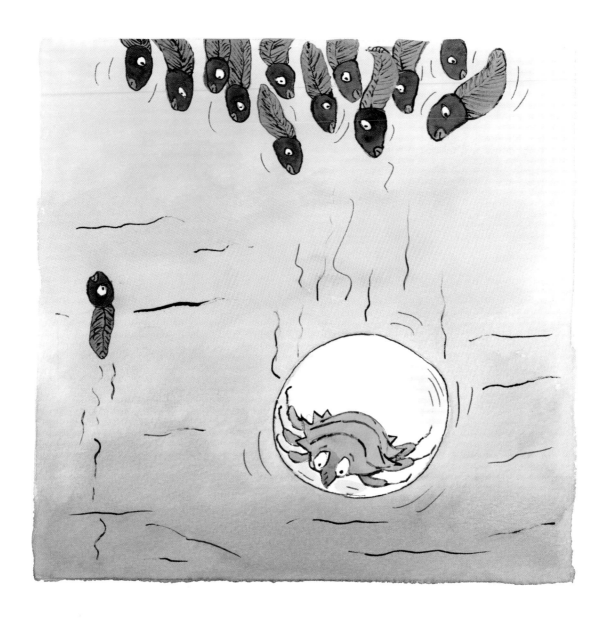

. . . to the bottom of the pond and his mother, Minnie, mad with worry . . .

"Thank goodness you're back!" She kissed him. "Where's your brother?" she yelled.

Then Ben told her everything and when he had finished Minnie put on her best hat and said, "Take me up. I must talk Boris out of this before it's too late!"

So Ben took Minnie up. And though Minnie liked it there
more than she would say, this was no time for enjoying herself.

She borrowed a table and two paddles and got Ben paddling
fast after Boris. But as fast as Ben paddled, the Boatman
paddled faster . . .

. . . and Boris got to Toptoad's territory before anyone could talk him out of it. And the Toptoads were watching. And the Toptoads were waiting . . .

"Going DOWN by any chance?" croaked Toptoad.
"DOWN?" spluttered Boris. But I just got UP. And while I'm here, I'd like to see round this top territory."

"Well, don't think you'll see inside our castle," said Lady Toptoad.
"I dropped the keys into the pond long ago and we can't even get
in ourselves."

"You could fetch the keys . . ." said Boris.

"From the bottom of the pond?" moaned Lady Toptoad. "We're the Toptoads. We don't go to the *bottom!*"

"Well, I'm Boris the Beetle," said Boris, "and I can go *anywhere* – bottom, middle, top. So it's no problem!"

Then to everyone's surprise, Boris, who'd just got up, went down. Down . . . down . . . down . . .

. . . down to the bottom of the pond, where he soon found the Toptoads' keys and brought them back up.

And the Toptoads were so grateful they gave him and his family half their castle.

But, though Boris was pleased, he didn't live there happily for the rest of his days. He lived EVERYWHERE for the rest of his days, moving easily between bottom, middle, top and top of the top.

Though it has to be said, once his mother moved into that half-a-castle, she wouldn't go *anywhere* . . . except over to the Toptoads' for tea . . . of course!